11/08

04/2013
1
10/2010

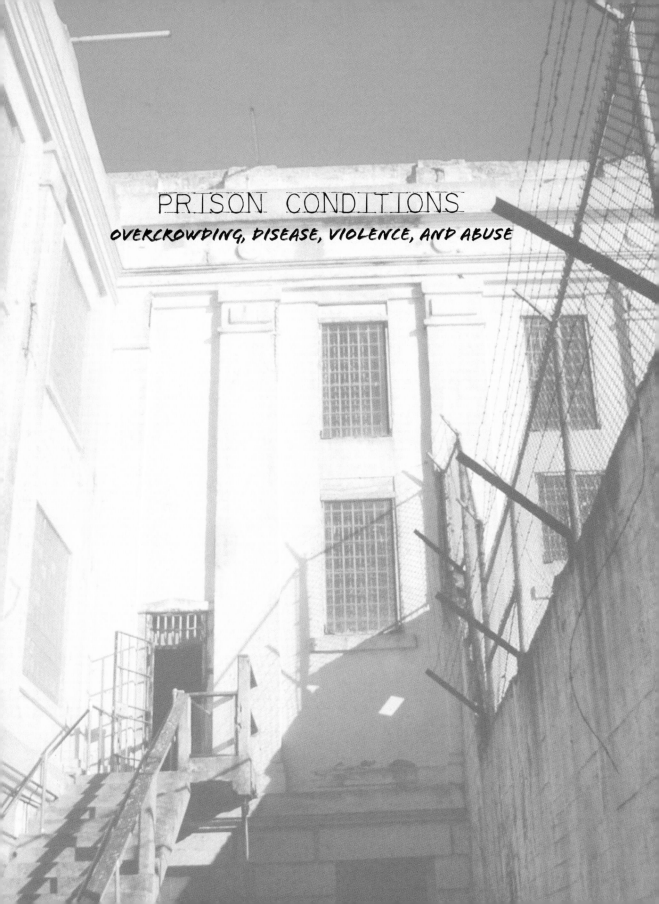

PRISON CONDITIONS

OVERCROWDING, DISEASE, VIOLENCE, AND ABUSE

Incarceration Issues:
Punishment, Reform, and Rehabilitation

TITLE LIST

PRISON CONDITIONS
OVERCROWDING DISEASE, VIOLENCE, AND ABUSE

by Roger Smith

Mason Crest Publishers
Philadelphia

Mason Crest Publishers Inc.
370 Reed Road
Broomall, Pennsylvania 19008
(866) MCP-BOOK (toll free)

2 3 4 5 6 7 8 9 10

Library of Congress Cataloging-in-Publication Data

Smith, Roger, 1959 Aug. 15–
  Prison conditions : overcrowding, disease, violence, and abuse / by
Roger Smith.
     p. cm. — (Incarceration issues)
  Includes bibliographical references and index.
  ISBN 1-59084-986-8   ISBN 1-59084-984-1 (series)
  ISBN 978-1-59084-986-6   ISBN 978-1-59084-984-2 (series)

  1. Prisons—United States—Juvenile literature. 2. Prisons—
Overcrowding—United States—Juvenile literature. 3. Prison violence—
United States—Juvenile literature. I. Title. II. Series.
  HV9471.R635 2007
  365.973—dc22
                    2006001476

Interior design by MK Bassett-Harvey.
Interiors produced by Harding House Publishing Service, Inc.
www.hardinghousepages.com

Cover design by Peter Spires Culotta.

Printed in Malaysia by Times Offset (M) Sdn.Bhd.

CONTENTS

INTRODUCTION

by Larry E. Sullivan, Ph.D.

Prisons will be with us as long as we have social enemies. We will punish them for acts that we consider criminal, and we will confine them in institutions.

Prisons have a long history, one that fits very nicely in the religious context of sin, evil, guilt, and expiation. In fact, the motto of one of the first prison reform organizations was "Sin no more." Placing offenders in prison was, for most of the history of the prison, a ritual for redemption through incarceration; hence the language of punishment takes on a very theological cast. The word "penitentiary" itself comes from the religious concept of penance. When we discuss prisons, we are dealing not only with the law but with very strong emotions and reactions to acts that range from minor or misdemeanor crimes to major felonies like murder and rape.

Prisons also reflect the level of the civilizing process through which a culture travels, and it tells us much about how we treat our fellow human beings. The great nineteenth-century Russian author Fyodor Dostoyevsky, who was a political prisoner, remarked, "The degree of civilization in a society can be measured by observing its prisoners." Similarly, Winston Churchill, the great British prime minister during World War II, said that the "treatment of crime and criminals is one of the most unfailing tests of civilization of any country."

Since the very beginnings of the American Republic, we have attempted to improve and reform the way we imprison criminals. For much of the history of the American prison, we tried to rehabilitate or modify the criminal behavior of offenders through a variety of treatment programs. In the last quarter of the twentieth century, politicians and citizens alike realized that this attempt had failed, and we began passing stricter laws, imprisoning people for longer terms and building more prisons. This movement has taken a great toll on society. Approximately two million people are behind bars today. This movement has led to the

overcrowding of prisons, worse living conditions, fewer educational programs, and severe budgetary problems. There is also a significant social cost, since imprisonment splits families and contributes to a cycle of crime, violence, drug addiction, and poverty.

All these are reasons why this series on incarceration issues is extremely important for understanding the history and culture of the United States. Readers will learn all facets of punishment: its history; the attempts to rehabilitate offenders; the increasing number of women and juveniles in prison; the inequality of sentencing among the races; attempts to find alternatives to incarceration; the high cost, both economically and morally, of imprisonment; and other equally important issues. These books teach us the importance of understanding that the prison system affects more people in the United States than any institution, other than our schools.

CHAPTER 1.

AN INTRODUCTION TO PRISON

What started as only a joke ended up ruining a life. He was only seventeen, about the age of the pretty girl behind the Photo Mat counter, and he wanted to say something funny to get her attention. He pulled out the toy gun found a few minutes earlier and told her, "Your money or your life," or something like that. She quickly turned around, opened the cash register, and gave him fifty-three dollars. Speechless, the boy took the money and ran home. The six-pack of beer he had that day

A condemned inmate at San Quentin Prison would face this long walk to his new housing.

WHAT ARE PRISONS?

Prisons vary in security: from double-barred steel cages inside high-walled, high-security fortresses to unlocked rooms in buildings surrounded by open fields. Prisoners' experiences of discomfort vary from living in windowless, tiny rooms with sensory-deprived isolation to living at work camps with no physical adversity. There are prisons that are like farms where prisoners spend their days working, unwatched, in the community. There are "weekend prisons" and "day prisons," and there are prisons with tediously boring routines broken only by flashes of violence and cruelty. There are prisons where the only exercise allowed is an hour of walking in an outdoor cage several times a week, and then there are prisons with tennis courts. There are prisons that are remarkably crowded and prisons of isolation. The most common prisons are overcrowded ones near large cities where the boring routines are interspersed with outbreaks of abuse and violence.

did not help his impulse control. His lawyer told him it did not matter that the gun was not real because as long as the girl behind the counter thought it was real, any judge would consider it armed robbery. The authorities gave the young man four and a half to fifteen years at Jackson Prison in southern Michigan—a facility holding 6,000 of the state's most violent prisoners.

He tried to look tough as he walked to 7 Block, but he did not look tough enough. Some older men pretending to be friendly invited him

Responsible and ethical prison guards can make all the difference in the conditions inmates face.

that first night to have some homemade liquor. They spiked it with Thorizine, and the boy became the evening's entertainment: the men gang-raped him. From that night on, one of the prisoners forced him to be his boy. He could not tell the guards because inmates kill snitches in prison. The **complacent** guards and administrators saw things and did nothing about them. The prisoner, who is now a free man, told the Stop Prison Rape (SPR) Web site,

> I wish you could see how I've paid for that stupid opening line and fifty three dollars over a quarter of a century ago. I wish I could allow you inside my experience for just a few minutes to see, and feel and fully understand the hell that lives with me every day . . . my shame, low self-esteem, self-hatred, deep-seated rage, and inability to trust have gone unabated for years.

According to SPR, inmates rape approximately one in ten males. SPR attributes this in part to the overcrowding and understaffing in many prisons.

BACKGROUND

Writers often use the terms "jail" and "prison" interchangeably when describing places of incarceration. Prisons are generally federal or state institutions that house convicted criminals serving long sentences, whereas cities or counties usually run jails. Authorities place people in jails who are awaiting a trial, a legal *disposition*, or serving a short sentence.

Different surveys report different numbers of people incarcerated, but all agree there are now more than two million U.S. citizens who are prisoners. According to Bill Moyer's report on PBS, "Prisons in America," in 1970, there were 338,029 inmates in the United States, but by mid-2004, the amount had soared to 2.1 million. The United States takes the lead for incarceration internationally with approximately 700 prisoners per 100,000 people; Russia follows in frequency of incarceration with 680 prisoners. Canada is eighth in the world at 116 prisoners. Both the United States and Canada have most Western and European countries beat where the incarceration rates per 100,000 are lower: Australia (110), Germany (95), Switzerland (90), and France (80).

Why the huge increase in the number of prisoners during the last few decades in the United States? According to Marc Mauer in *Americans Behind Bars: U.S. and International Use of Incarceration*, one cause might be a high rate of violent crime for which the country believes offenders should be imprisoned. Another cause could be stiffer punishments than those given for similar crimes in other nations.

Norval Morris, in *The Oxford History of the Prison*, suggests that the rise in U.S. imprisonment is largely because of sentencing reforms. Because of a rise in crime during the late 1960s and early 1970s, a mentality of "get tough on crime" caused more criminals to be sentenced to prison for longer terms, and stiffer policies for drug arrests came into being. According to the FBI, almost 60 percent of federal prisoners were in

PRISON CONDITIONS

During the 1980s, judges became "tougher on crime."

> *"If only there were evil people somewhere insidiously committing evil deeds, and it were necessary only to separate them from the rest of us and destroy them. But the line dividing good and evil cuts through the heart of every human being and who is willing to destroy his (or her) own heart?"*
>
> —Alexander Solzhenitsyn, former political prisoner in Russia

prison for drug-related offenses by mid-2001. "Three strikes and you're out" laws for repeat offenders and "truth in sentencing" laws restricting early release also raised the prison population. Where once a parole board could release a prisoner at an earlier date than his maximum sentence, this became less likely in the 1980s. The public accused judges and parole boards of being too soft on criminals; consequently, parole officers began cracking down on parolees—oftentimes returning them to prison at the first sign of a parole offense. Through the 1980s, the public experienced a growing fear of crime. Politicians noticed they could boost their popularity by opposing crime because no powerful group of voters is usually against a "get tough on crime agenda."

WHO'S WHO IN PRISON?

The two main groups involved in prison life are the prisoners and the staff. Each sees the other with some prejudice. Inmates view guards as stupid and *authoritarian*, and correctional officers see prisoners as corrupt, untrustworthy, and vicious.

Most prisoners are male.

Prisoners and staff often view each other with distrust.

The average age of inmates in the United States is thirty-seven years old. In the federal prisons, 92 percent are male. Fifty percent are white, and the rest are black, Native American, Asian, Hispanic, or "other." The Federal Bureau of Prisons (FBOP) lists 70 percent of U.S. inmates as American; 20 percent as Colombian, Mexican, or Cuban; and 10 percent as coming from other countries. Fifty-eight percent are incarcerated for drug offenses.

Aging prisoners are a growing population. In the state of Arizona, by the year 2009, more than 2,000 graying inmates will be behind bars, and the state must pay for all their medical needs. Arizona is a mirror of a national problem: states are trying to find ways to pay for the mounting

AN INTRODUCTION TO PRISON

Race plays an important role in prison.

PRISON TERMS

The following is a glossary of slang used in prison.

ace boon coon: A prisoner's best buddy.
all day: A life sentence.
fresh fish: New prisoners.
badge: A prison guard.
bug: An insane person who annoys other prisoners.
catnap: A short prison term.
snitch: A prisoner who tells the guards information on other prisoners.

medical costs of aging prison populations. Approximately sixteen states have special housing units for **geriatric** inmates.

Prisoners find out quickly that the main dividing line in the institution is race. Black prisoners stay with blacks, whites stay with whites, and Hispanics stay with Hispanics. If one strays into the other's turf, especially in facilities with very violent criminals, they may be beaten, raped, or killed.

Several subcultures can be found in prison. One group is international drug smugglers who do not see themselves as "criminals." Among this group are Cubans, Mexicans, Colombians, and Jamaicans. Another subgroup is made up of members of organized crime, which includes the Mafia. A third group is the bikers, which may include Hell's Angels, Pagans, Outlaws, Diablos, Satan's Slaves, and other motorcycle clubs. Thousands of these bikers are imprisoned.

On any cellblock of 500 prisoners, a couple of dozen or so will be violent sociopaths.

CORRECTIONAL OFFICERS' DIFFICULT JOB

A correctional officer's job is not easy. Authors Ross and Richards describe a typical cellblock: "In every cellblock (typically 500 prisoners) there are a couple dozen seething **paranoids** and violent **sociopaths** who've armed themselves with deadly weapons." Gangs in prison keep guards on the constant lookout for violent outbreaks. Gang members **coerce** guards to smuggle drugs into prison for them: they have a friend on the outside take a picture of the guard's family and home, then show the

Violence is all too common in prison.

photo and threaten violence to his family if he doesn't smuggle drugs to the gang.

Correctional officers often work long hours and are poorly paid. The job is one of the less desirable in law enforcement, and the best way for a guard to make a respectable income is to put in long hours of overtime. Many guards are stressed out, burned out, and cynical; most of them just want to get through their day with no problems. Usually, the only time the public notices correctional officers is when there is a prison riot or an escape.

One writer, Ted Conover, who made it his mission to get inside the experience of a correctional officer, believes there are good guards and bad guards, and that the profession is misunderstood and underappreciated. Conover did not want to excuse abuse, but to help the public understand it in the context of a brutal system, he became a correctional officer at Sing Sing prison. He didn't tell his superiors or other guards about his project; they had no idea that he would be writing about his experience.

While Conover worked at Sing Sing, the job transformed him. Every morning when he woke up, he wondered if he would be hurt that day. He couldn't do the job and not jump in if a friend was in trouble. He began wanting to use brute strength against prisoners after seeing them attack other guards and disobey orders. He found prison to be full of frustration with very little outlet for the stress; the more he did the job, the more he wanted to use force: it felt like a release, a cleansing. He was torn between his duties as a correctional officer and as a person.

He tells of following a prisoner overburdened with laundry bags, wanting to help him—but officers are not allowed to help prisoners. A civilian passing by criticized him, and so feeling guilty, he helped the prisoner—but then the other guards **berated** him. In the end, he felt like he was neither a good guard nor a good person.

Conover found that correctional officers had many marital problems, and divorce was common among them. He thought that he could keep from having these difficulties, but he found that he became distant from his wife, becoming moody and silent. He tried to keep the horrors from

There are good guards and bad guards.

her and his family, so he separated himself from them. When he came home having done things that made him feel dirty, he would act differently around his family and friends. It was a **stigmatized** job that involved actions so shameful that they were hidden out of sight.

Eventually, Ted Conover wrote a book called *Life as a Jailor*, describing his experience. Even after leaving his life as a guard, however, he dreams about the prison several times a week.

According to Jeffrey Ian Ross, who worked for more than three years in a correctional facility, and Stephen C. Richards, who spent eleven years in federal custody, the authors of *Behind Bars: Surviving Prison*, some guards are honorable and decent people, while others are not. A number of them come to work every day and treat prisoners with courtesy and respect. Some have earned the nicknames of "hacks" and "cops." A

Many prisoners have committed crimes that merit them being locked away from the rest of society.

"hack" is an officer who does as little as possible, collects his paycheck, and goes home. A "cop" is a guard who is constantly trying to catch prisoners breaking petty rules. They will send prisoners to the hole (solitary confinement) "and another officer, a man who deserves your thanks, will get you out." The best guards are women and men who are level headed and treat prisoners with care. A few correctional officers have risked their jobs and the anger of other guards and administrators to stand up for the rights of inmates.

VICTIMS OF PRISONERS

"I hope that someone will realize that the victims are the *true* prisoners . . . NOT the criminals. . . . I only wish the rapist would understand that I am in prison for the rest of my life. There is no parole. There is no time off for good behavior."

A woman wrote these words after she was raped and almost murdered. Her date was walking her to her apartment one night, when a man put a knife to his throat and forced the two into her apartment. She endured the next five hours of torture with a hunting knife and extreme sexual torture by a heroin addict.

She never got over it, although she has spent thousands and thousands of dollars on therapies, trying to ease her emotional trauma. She has seen the best doctors, taken medication, and joined **twelve-step groups**. She is a religious person and forgives the man who did this, but nothing numbs the pain; she has never been able to get over it. She says she is permanently damaged, and that will never change.

A father from Florida wrote to the Dark Sorrow Web site about a family friend who began molesting the father's two small sons when they were four and five years old. The molestation went on for two years until the man was found out, stopped, and sentenced to eleven consecutive life sentences. The police found in his possession a self-written manuscript on how to seduce, molest, and kill a child and make it look like an accident. Fortunately, the Florida boys were found before they were killed. The father writes in anger because the Web site expresses sympathy for both victims and criminals in prison. He says, "Do you feel sorrow for this man who will spend the rest of his life in prison? Do you really care if atrocities against him by other inmates may happen? Will you feel sorrow if he were murdered in that prison? I answer no to all of the above. . . . Now we have our life sentences to try and straighten out our boys' lives."

Tragedies such as these have occurred in the lives of many in North America. Our prisons have countless inmates living out the rest of their years in prison for destroying the lives of other people. Some members

Prisoners' suffering cannot be divorced from the rest of society.

of the general public feel prisoners deserve to suffer the rest of their lives and that poor prison conditions are what they deserve.

REHABILITATION VS. PUNISHMENT

Although Canada also has many problems concerning incarceration, Canadian society places a higher priority on rehabilitating inmates. As stated by the Correctional Services of Canada (CSC), the primary reason for imprisoning criminals in Canada is for the security of the general population. Since the prison population will eventually be released, the second goal of prison is to prepare inmates to return to society as law-abiding citizens—to **rehabilitate** them to live productive lives in society.

The authors of *Behind Bars: Surviving Prison* believe that many prison administrators in the United States have given up on rehabilitation; instead, "they devote their budgets to cement, bricks, and steel to build more facilities to house a growing prisoner population." These authors believe that most wardens seem to have limited their efforts to the safety and custody problems of their prisons. Thankfully, they say, some prison staff come to work each day and try to help individual prisoners, through conversation, operating specific programs, or setting a good example. They find fulfillment in assisting inmates to grow and learn the skills and attitudes needed to live useful, law-abiding lives.

Some citizens think that efforts to rehabilitate prisoners such as college courses, parenting classes, vocational training, and psychological therapy are undeserved privileges for lawbreakers, whereas others see rehabilitation as a way to reform convicts and reduce crime. Whether in Canada or the United States, the treatment of inmates ultimately affects the rest of society. Prisons in the United States release 500,000 prisoners every year. If overcrowding, disease, violence, and abuse are rampant in prisons, and if these conditions irreparably harm the men and women who eventually return to society, then society suffers.

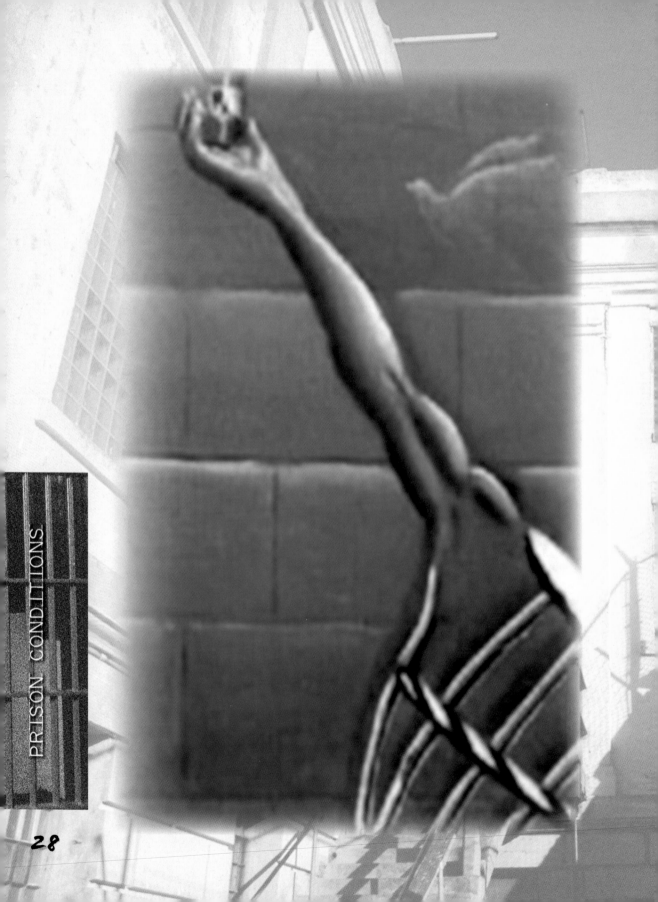

CHAPTER 2

OVERCROWDING: TOO MANY PRISONERS IN ONE PLACE

One day the world of Victor Hassine, author of *Life Without Parole: Living in Prison Today,* suddenly turned upside down. Without warning, his cell door opened and prison guards sent another man inside. Victor had been in Pennsylvania's prison system for over twelve years and was doing well, as he put it, in his routine of "working, obeying and vegetating." He had been in a single cell until that day.

The first argument the cellmates had was over who got the top or bottom bunk. Next, they fought over when they would turn the lights on or off, toilet hygiene habits, property storage, cell cleaning, and when friends could visit. Every day they argued over missing property. Their waking hours were filled with accusations of stealing, snoring, bodily noises, or smoking—and every day they found something more to argue about.

Hassine's experiences were not unique. As prisons became more crowded, authorities placed prisoners together based merely on their race or age or cell availability. Inmates did not have the chance to interview potential cellmates. Living so closely together, differences between individuals were bound to grate on each other's nerves.

WHAT IS "OVERCROWDING"?

Victor Hassine says the term "prison overcrowding" is an overused term describing a collection of conditions that disrupt prisons all over the United States. He says such words do not make the reality clear to the public. The public usually sees it as a vague "social problem," a softened term that does not define the "extreme, hopeless, horrifying, and tragic conditions that truly exist. The blood and guts of what prison overcrowding is inside and what it really does to the insiders remains an **enigma** to most outsiders."

Jimmy Lerner, author of the book *You Got Nothing Coming*, describes his cell in a Nevada state prison: it was eight by six feet with a twelve-foot ceiling, a fluorescent lightbulb with a mesh screen around it, and a stainless-steel toilet (with no cover) connected to a sink unit. The cinder block walls in his cell were yellow-brown from years of cigarette smoke, and there was much "moronic graffiti." He says, "I've always had a mild case of claustrophobia, but until cell 47 in the Fish Tank [in prison jargon, fish are prisoners, and the prison is the fish tank] it had never been more than a minor inconvenience. With the beds jutting out three feet from the wall, only one man at a time could comfortably stand up." He had heard of the chronic problem of prison overcrowding before, but the

In many correctional facilities, more than one prisoner must live in a single cell.

issue seemed as far removed from his life as the atrocities reported in the Balkans. He goes on to say, "The issue had a bit more immediacy now."

In many correctional facilities, prisoners are double bunked in cells meant for one person. In some prisons, inmates sleep in cold prison gyms or on the floors of basements, halls, and dayrooms. Some prisons use tents or sleep prisoners in the same bunks at different times of the day.

Overcrowding is a concern in Canadian prisons as well. The Canadian Church Council on Justice and Corrections Web site tells of an incident in a Toronto jail where authorities housed three men convicted of a violent armed robbery in pretrial custody for approximately ten months in a six- by nine-foot jail cell meant for single occupancy. Authorities allowed for a shorter sentence because of the difficult, overcrowded conditions. Not only were the cells too small for three men, but guards only allowed the three to go outside for recreation once a week. The rules

Imagine sharing this tiny space with another human being!

stipulate that authorities should let prisoners out for twenty minutes a day, but due to understaffing, this was impossible.

STATISTICS

According to *Prisons and Jails: A Deterrent to Crime?*, U.S. federal prisons were at 26 percent above capacity in 1995 and 31 percent over capacity in 2000. Overcrowding is also an issue in juvenile residential facilities. In 2000, 39 percent of juvenile detention centers had more residents than available beds. Most states reported having some overcrowding in their facilities. Wyoming had the least overcrowding with 17 percent of facilities, and Massachusetts had the most at 77 percent with overcrowding.

Canada has its overcrowding problems as well. According to Statistics Canada, in 2002–2003, the population of adult prisoners in provincial or territorial jails fell by 3 percent; in 1996, Canada began to allow more offenders facing incarceration to serve their time in the community under specified conditions, and this accounts for the decline in confined prisoners. Unfortunately, however, the number of prisoners on remand—in jails waiting for a court appearance—has risen since the 1980s: there is a courtroom-overcrowding problem. On average, 8,700 prisoners were on remand in territorial or provincial jails on any given day, a 70 percent increase since 1993–1994.

REASONS FOR OVERCROWDING

Between 1970 and 1994, U.S. state and federal lawmakers made a big change in sentencing practices. In the 1960s, laws set the maximum time a person could serve in prison for different offenses. A judge could sentence a person to less than this amount but not more, and a parole board later decided the actual time a prisoner would serve. The parole board made its decision when to release the prisoner based on the severity of the person's crime, how well she behaved in prison, and how well the

board thought the person would do in society. Released prisoners would then have a certain amount of time to be on parole after getting out of prison. Prison terms were not set in concrete because the basic belief was that incarceration would reform the prisoner. If a prisoner accepted help in prison from the available educational, vocational, and psychological training, authorities might release him at an earlier date.

During the late 1960s and early 1970s, however, attitudes changed. A series of articles published in the United States claimed that prisoners were unable to be reformed; the idea that a criminal could not change became popular. At the same time, crime increased, and lawmakers and politicians began to believe greater punishments could stop this trend. The press portrayed judges and parole boards as being too easy on criminals. Reformers recommended that governments eliminate parole

During the 1970s, judges began handing down "mandatory sentences."

POLICE DISCRIMINATION

Evidence indicates that racial minorities still suffer discrimination at the hands of the police. Officers are more likely to shoot, kill, arrest, or physically abuse people of color. Officers who are guilty of these behaviors often do not receive punishment for their misdeeds.

boards and make prisoners serve mandatory sentences. Legislatures and judges agreed on "truth in sentencing." This meant that an inmate would have to serve her full sentence. The criminal would not serve only a small fraction of her term, or be released on parole after sentencing, or have her sentence commuted to **probation** and serve none of her time. Then, in the 1980s, authorities cut rehabilitation programs in prisons and social services for parolees. Although crime rates in the 1990s were slightly lower than in the 1980s, the rates of imprisonment increased because of these sentencing reforms.

Parole boards are still in place in the prison system. If an inmate has served his minimum sentence, a parole board reviews his case to decide if he is ready for society. If the board thinks a release is acceptable, it comes up with a release plan. This plan will often specify that the person keep free of drugs and alcohol, stay away from other ex-offenders, and remain employed. He must report regularly to a parole officer, and if a parolee violates terms or commits any new crime, authorities will return him to prison.

According to Kelly Virella, one of the authors of *Prison Nation: The Warehousing of America's Poor*, parole officers have a stake in catching parolees who violate the conditions of their release. To keep their jobs, they have to catch offenders and put them back in prison. Some officers show lenience and fairness, but many officers reincarcerate at the first sign that an ex-prisoner has violated his parole conditions. Over 50 percent of men released from prison return within the first year and 70 percent within three years. Many parolees are returned to prison for technical violations of parole rules such as failure to report to their officer, being unemployed, testing positive for illegal drugs, or not paying court costs.

There are also many possible reasons for the increase in the Canadian prison population. Some Canadian experts feel their justice system relies excessively on imprisonment rather than other options. Another reason for the increase in prison population is that the public has taken on a punishing attitude toward offenders rather than a rehabilitative one. During the last decade, social and mental health services have been reduced, which may lead to more criminal behaviors. Communities are becoming less tolerant of crime so they are giving inmates longer sentences and even life sentences.

RACIAL OVERCROWDING

The authors of *The Color of Justice: Race, Ethnicity and Crime in America*, Samuel Walker, Cassia Spohn, and Miriam DeLone, say that nearly 60 percent of U.S. prison and jail inmates were ethnic or racial minorities in 2004. About 12.6 percent of all black men age twenty-five to twenty-nine were in jails or prisons. For Hispanics, it was 3.6 percent, and for white men in that age group it was 1.7 percent.

Blacks are arrested at an unusually high rate compared to whites for violent crimes such as murder, rape, and robbery. The criminal justice process treats minorities more severely than white offenders; an example of this is the greater likelihood that minorities will receive the death penalty. In some regions of the country, police departments tolerate ex-

Many prison inmates are black.

cessive force directed at racial minorities. Authorities tend to treat members of racial minorities who are young, male, unemployed, and convicted of violent crimes or drug offenses more harshly than whites who commit these crimes or have these characteristics.

Judges may have racial prejudice.

Research shows that times have changed. Before the 1960s, **blatant** discrimination ruled. Walker, Spohn, and DeLone do not believe that society has erased racial bigotry from the justice system, but it has diminished. In the twenty-first century, if a white man commits a crime against a black man, he is not above the law, and if a black man commits a crime against a white man, he will not receive justice at the hand of a white **lynch mob**.

Research shows that discrimination exists in the court system as well. Some judges give harsher sentences to black offenders who murder or rape whites and more lenient sentences if the crime was against a fellow black. In some cases, people of color are more likely to get prison, whereas whites may only get probation. In part because of these discriminatory sentencing practices, a much larger number of blacks are incarcerated in U.S. jails and prisons.

EFFECTS OF OVERCROWDING

Overcrowding affects all the other issues of prison life—disease, violence, and abuse. Willie Wilson, an author included in *Prison Nation: The Warehousing of America's Poor,* writes that most prison inmates have histories of drug and alcohol use, and have been victims of sexual, emotional, and physical abuse. They do not come to prison with "highly developed coping mechanisms" and cannot get away from the stress around them to be alone and reflect or think. Many of them are mentally ill; in California alone, there are 20,000 mentally ill prisoners. When all these prisoners are overcrowded, the effects can be devastating. Kara Gotsch, public policy coordinator of the National Prison Project, says, "Overcrowding is one component that contributes to many different problems."

Prison overcrowding in Saskatchewan, Canada, has been a growing issue for many years. The effects are numerous. Overcrowding increases tensions, as it is harder to keep incompatible inmates separate. With so many inmates, each individual has fewer programming opportunities; sometimes, prison officials have to use large program rooms as dormitories for the extra prisoners. More inmates must serve their time away from hometowns, and family visits are not as frequent because of this. Several facilities in the province have had to go to double bunking; privacy is almost nonexistent when a person must share not only a cell but a bed.

Due to overcrowding in an Oregon prison, authorities moved seventy-eight women to an Arizona detention center. The new prison was mostly a men's facility and lacked a separate unit for women. Instead, the prison used a medical quarantine room close to the hospital area for this purpose. According to five women in this group, guards sexually abused

women for months, and no one stopped the abuse. The situation started when a guard captain gave six women marijuana joints. He returned with several other guards and told the women that these officers would search their cells. To avoid charges of possession for marijuana, the correctional officers forced the women to perform a strip tease. In the end, fifty guards were involved in the incident—from starting the abuse to covering it up. They transported five of the women back to Oregon in an attempt to keep the matter quiet, but one of the women told her story to *Prison Legal News*. Five women eventually filed a suit in Tucson against the prison and fifteen employees. According to the book *Prison Nation*, **degradation** of this sort is common in prisons.

When officials confine too many prisoners to a space, sanitation also declines, and inmates become more susceptible to disease. Prison experts also believe that overcrowding is distressing to inmates, which leads to violence. Kara Gotsch says, "Prisons are very violent, unsafe and damaging places. A person goes in and is never the same."

Because of crowding, Pleasant Valley State Prison houses level-three prisoners (inmates with longer sentences, prior prison terms, or special behavior problems) in a gymnasium where they sleep in triple bunk beds with little space between each bed. In 2003, a riot involving 300 inmates broke out in one of the gymnasiums. A guard shot and killed a twenty-eight-year-old prisoner who was serving fifteen years to life for second-degree murder.

SOLUTIONS

Both the United States and Canada agree that one of the main ways to stop prison overcrowding is to send fewer people to prison. The Canadian Criminal Justice Association (CCJA) has called on all criminal justice authorities and the public to consider how to decrease overcrowding in Canadian prisons and jails. A number of jurisdictions are already working to make changes. CCJA is encouraging the communities to try more tactics of crime prevention. They are advocating that authorities use imprisonment as one of several options—not the only option. CCJA

PRISON CONDITIONS

THE CONVICT CODE

The following is a list of dos and don'ts that prisoners should follow if they want to survive among other inmates.

Don't:
- Attract attention.
- Break your promises.
- Snitch on other prisoners.
- Lose your head.
- Take advantage of fellow convicts.
- Pressure other prisoners.

Do:
- Be loyal to prisoners as a group.
- Be honorable.
- Pay any debts.
- Be a man.
- Mind your own business.
- Play it cool.
- Do your own time.
- Watch your words.
- Be aware at all times.
- Be tough.

Community service and work release programs are forms of alternative sentencing.

hopes that authorities will work more to help inmates successfully reintegrate into society. This may decrease the return rate of prisoners.

The Human Rights Watch group in the United States also believes solutions can be found to prison overcrowding. This group wants states to reexamine their sentencing policies: shorter sentences for prisoners might be wise, fair, and more cost-effective. Human Rights Watch encourages the total elimination of mandatory minimum sentences and asks courts to consider alternatives to imprisonment. The group's view is that incarceration is often unnecessary and damages many inmates. Group members are working to persuade officials to consider their recommendations and make the necessary changes.

Alternative forms of sentencing are now widely used in many states. Instead of prison, authorities are offering some first-time offenders a choice of alternative sentences. Some of these include **boot camp**, community service programs, fines, day reporting centers, work release,

weekend sentencing**, **electronic monitoring**, **house arrest, and residential community corrections.

Canada has used alternative sentencing for years; it refers to this practice as "sentencing options." The most common option is a fine: authorities fine 45 percent of the adult offenders eligible for sentencing alternatives. Probation, ***restitution***, community service, conditional sentence (community service), and intermittent imprisonment such as weekend prison are some of the other alternative sentences used to help keep prison crowding down.

Unfortunately, overcrowding continues to be an all-too real issue for North American prisoners. It contributes to many other problems, including the spread of diseases between prisoners. In a population prone to mental illnesses, overcrowding intensifies these problems as well.

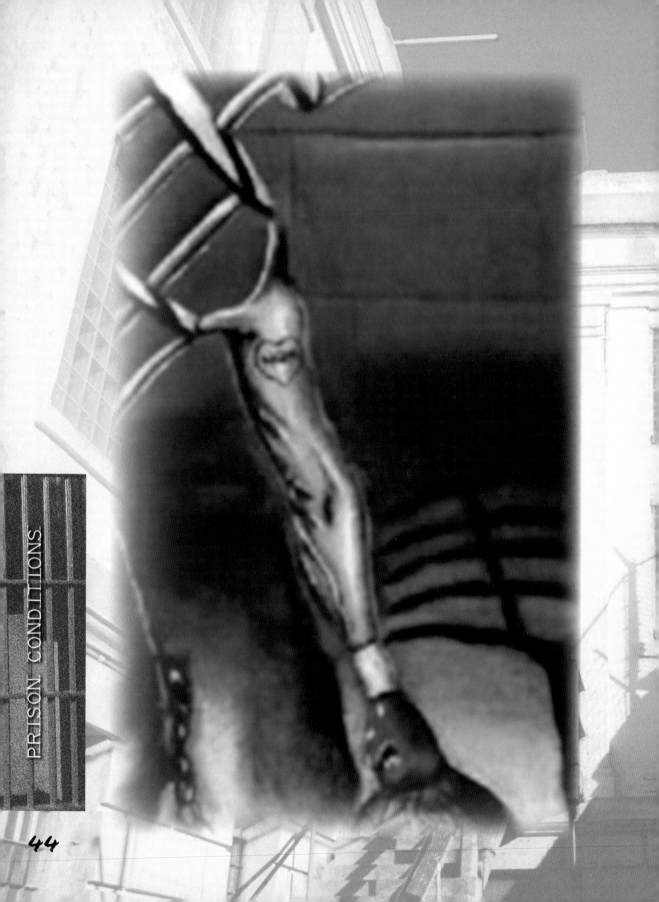

44

CHAPTER 3

DISEASE

At Lancaster Prison in California, a prisoner walks his dog every day, tugging at the leash in a zigzag pattern across the prison yard. His bloodshot eyes glance wildly as he talks continuously to his little dog. The other men sneer and make fun of him as he shuffles by. They don't pet the dog because it is not really there.

Before starting his day, the dog-owner gets out of bed, beats his chest to kill the wicked pig living in there, and stuffs all his important papers in his waistband. He goes for weeks without a shower. When he leaves the cafeteria, he spins around and knocks three times on the table before leaving. He has conversations with people only he can see, often cursing and spitting. He is one of 20,000 mentally ill prisoners in California state prisons—and as author Willie Wilson put it, "They're driving the other 162,000 prisoners crazy."

Prisoners with mental illnesses are often inadequately treated or not treated at all due to shortages in qualified staff members and specialized facilities. Prisoners with more traditional illnesses fare little better. For example, at California's Pleasant Valley State Prison when an inmate became ill, his condition was not even correctly diagnosed for several weeks. His wife confided to the *Fresno Bee* newspaper how guards pushed him along with other prisoners through the medical care facility "like cattle" and then the doctor told him it was just a cold. Later, other doctors told him it was pneumonia, but eventually, doctors determined he was suffering from Valley Fever, an illness spread by a fungus. Despite what is shown in these examples, all prisoners have the constitutional right to receive proper medical care, whether psychiatric care or general health care.

In many cases, prison medical workers have lost their rights to practice medicine in outside society. Some doctors have had their medical licenses revoked, or have been convicted of a crime in other states. In an overcrowded system, the staff often believes that prisoners' medical requests are attention-seeking behaviors or a way to get drugs; therefore, staff ignores some medical requests. Prisons have an overall pattern of poor health care, and this neglect affects the lives of prisoners and may eventually affect society in general when authorities release these inmates.

PRISON CONDITIONS

MENTALLY ILL PATIENTS

Approximately one in every six prisoners in the United States is mentally ill and many suffer from serious illnesses such as ***schizophrenia***, depres-

A prisoner with mental illness is not likely to receive the treatment he needs.

sion, or **bipolar disorder.** Human Rights Watch found that most mentally ill prisoners are not adequately treated or not treated at all. Some mentally ill prisoners who are undertreated or untreated suffer painful symptoms: they curl up silently in their cells; babble, rant, and *rail*; or they hallucinate and live in invisible worlds. They cover themselves in feces, pound their heads against walls, and self-mutilate their bodies. Some of them commit suicide. In many prisons, the facilities are not specialized for mental illness and there is a shortage of staff.

The Canadian PsychLinks Online Web site cites an internal study by Corrections Canada, reporting that the justice system is incarcerating an increasing number of mentally ill patients in federal prisons where inadequate treatment is available. Studies show that in 2004, 11 percent of new prisoners had a mental disorder, whereas in 1997 only 7 percent had a mental health issue. The Corrections Canada Report stated that although the number of total federal prisoners is dropping, the number of

Prisons were not built to handle the special needs of inmates who have mental illnesses.

Homeless people with mental illnesses often end up in prison.

mentally ill inmates is rising. Officials did not design the system to serve them, and so it is not able to respond correctly to their needs.

How did so many people with mental illness end up in prison? In the United States, it started in the 1960s with a process called "deinstitutionalization," when mental health institutions released many of their patients. The originators of this idea imagined that community-based mental health services would be in place to help these released patients, but the services were never set up. In the end, deinstitutionalization meant that a flood of homeless people with mental illnesses or addictions roamed city streets, unable to find help. When they went untreated, their emotional stability went downhill quickly, and many ended up breaking the law.

Canada also went through a cost-cutting phase with mental health facilities. In the 1990s, many provincial mental health institutions released

Women with emotional problems also face extreme challenges within prison walls.

patients. The results have been a shifting of former patients over to prisons—so prisons are merely reinstitutionalizing mentally ill patients.

Once people with mental illnesses become criminal offenders in the United States, they face a system that sends people to prison even for low-level, nonviolent crimes. Human Rights Watch believes U.S. prisons are not set up for the special needs of the mentally ill, so these patients are often victims of violence and *extortion* by other inmates or guards. When a prisoner with mental illness breaks the rules too many times, guards put him in solitary confinement where he spends up to twenty-four hours in a small, sometimes windowless cell. Long periods of solitary confinement are hard to endure for people who are healthy, but such treatment can cause mentally ill prisoners to break down completely. When that happens, authorities take them to psychiatric hospitals for treatment, but they often return to solitary confinement—and the cycle begins all over again.

The Canadian Association of Elizabeth Fry Society (CAEFS) has a mission to help criminalized women and girls in the justice system. Kim Pate, CAEFS' executive director and a teacher and lawyer, shares her experience in a Web article called "Prisons as Panacea." As a student, she volunteered to tutor female prisoners and psychiatric patients. When she started out, she had no idea how many days and nights for the next twenty years she would spend kneeling in front of metal doors and meal slots trying to help prisoners. She found some prisoners slashing their bodies, shackled, or banging their heads against the wall. "Nor could I have imagined the utter disdain with which others, be they correctional authorities, members of parliament, or academics might regard calls for the law to be upheld in the treatment of prisoners."

Pate cites the downsizing of mental health facilities as a major reason for the incarceration of a growing number of women with psychological disabilities. She says that when officials put these women out on the streets, their efforts to survive, self-medicate, and cope often lead them down the wrong avenues and into prisons.

HELP IS ON THE WAY

An important milestone in prison mental health in the United States occurred on October 30, 2004, when President George W. Bush signed the Mentally Ill Offender Treatment and Crime Reduction Act. The act gave fifty million dollars in grant money to help make sure juvenile and adult nonviolent offenders with mental illness receive correct diagnoses and receive the treatment they need from the time of their arrest until their release into the community. The grant will also help establish more mental health courts and give more funds for pretrial *jail diversion programs*. Resources will also go to improve the overall quality of mental health care in prisons and jails.

The Canadian National Committee for Police/Mental Health Liaison (CNCPMHL) is an organization of police officers and mental health professionals providing information, services, and support to police

officers. Since police officers are the first officials who make contact with offenders who have a mental illness, they can benefit from special training. The main goal of the CNCPMHL is to help guard against the unnecessary "criminalization" of the mentally ill. The committee teaches police how to direct offenders to the system that is best for them in their circumstances. For example, if a crime has been committed, police might direct an offender to the criminal justice system—but if the person was clearly not a danger to society, she might instead be sent to the mental health system for treatment. In some cases, offenders might be released if they are not dangerous and they so choose.

PRISONERS WITH HIV

In case after case I reviewed, prisoners were deliberately denied the standard medical treatment for HIV infection. It is my professional opinion that the grossly inappropriate care currently being provided is resulting in unnecessary pain and suffering and will be responsible for unnecessary deaths for patients who would respond to appropriate treatment.

This is the testimony of Dr. Robert Cohen for the plaintiffs in a case concerning the Mississippi State Prison (MSP) Parchman Farm. Author Anne-Marie Cusac quotes him in *Prison Nation: The Warehousing of America's Poor*. Dr. Cohen has been the director of the Montefiore Rikers Island Health Service in New York State, overseeing the care of 13,000 inmates. He has also reviewed medical care for the Department of Justice.

In 1999, Parchman became involved in a lawsuit filed by HIV-positive patients. Patients claimed that the medical care they were receiving was threatening their lives. The issue revolved mainly around the drugs prescribed at the prison. Since 1996, the basic government recommendation for AIDS and HIV medications urged a three-drug combination therapy; using one or two drugs was greatly discouraged. Some state incarceration facilities, however, such as MSP Parchman, do not allow three-drug treatments. At Parchman, the rules required prisoners to take two-drug

HIV-positive inmates often do not receive the treatment they need.

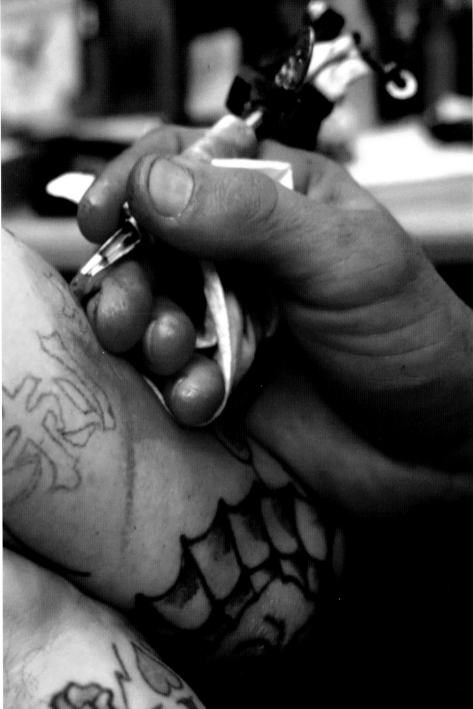

"Tatting" is just one way that prisoners may be exposed to contaminated needles that could transmit HIV or other diseases.

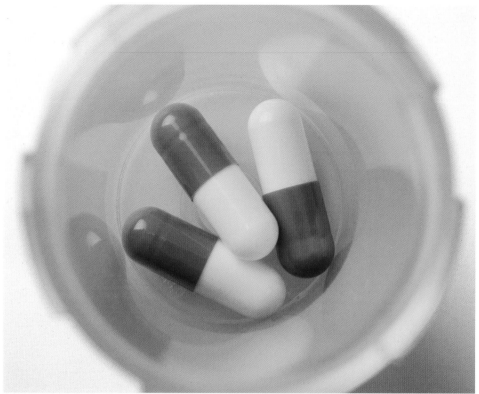
Receiving the correct regimen of drugs is important to their effectiveness.

therapy for six months before officials allowed the third drug (called a protease inhibitor). If the prisoner had been on three drugs successfully before coming to prison, it did not matter; they had to go back on two. Dr. Cohen reported that adding a third drug to two failing drugs is usually proven to start an early development of resistance to HIV drugs. "This is almost always the wrong approach, and it is the only approach taken at MSP Parchman," wrote Dr. Cohen. Unfortunately, the policies at Parchman are common in U.S. prisons.

An inmate in the Florida prison system came to prison HIV positive, and officials gave him his medications. However, he received them at mealtime. The prisoner had carefully researched medications before serving his time, and he knew he had to wait an hour after taking the pills to eat because they were 77 percent less effective if he took them with food. Given prison procedures, he had the choice of skipping his

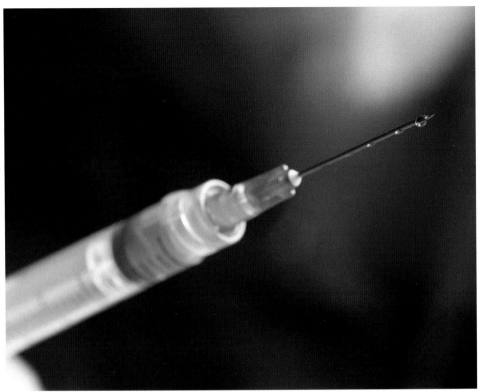

When inmates who use drugs share needles, HIV can spread through prisons.

breakfast to save his health or making his illness worse. The medications also came at the wrong time at night, so he kept the pills in his mouth and then put them into his pocket to take later. This was risky behavior; authorities could have locked him up in disciplinary confinement for trying to stay alive—yet taking the medications in the wrong way could have killed him. The American Civil Liberties Union helped find a solution to the problem. After serving his time in the prison system, his comment was, "The judge gave me ten years, he didn't sentence me to death."

The AIDS Foundation of Chicago estimates the AIDS rate in U.S. prisons is fourteen times higher than in the general population. In a 1991 report, the National Commission on AIDS stated that by choosing mass imprisonment as the federal and state response for drug offenders, the prison system is getting more and more inmates with HIV. In 2001, 57 percent of incarcerations were for drug offenses. According to the HIV InSite Web site, 20 to 26 percent (180,000 to 235,000) of people living with AIDS in the United Sates have been in jails or prisons.

Canadian prison populations also struggle with HIV/AIDS. According to the Canadian HIV/AIDS Legal Network, the HIV count in federal prisons rose from 14 infected inmates in 1989 to 251 in 2002. In provincial prisons, a study done in Quebec, Ontario, and British Columbia resulted in findings that HIV infections are ten times higher than the rate in the general public.

The HIV/AIDS Legal Network in Canada says that overall, most Canadian prisons provide good care for patients with HIV/AIDS and many times send them to outside sources for care. However, some patients say the care they receive is below public standards. Some Canadian prisons are not well equipped to deal with inmates who need long-term care, nor can they handle the increasing number of patients who are ill. Prisons also have difficulty getting experimental drugs and alternative therapies.

What's more, prison exposes inmates to AIDS in a variety of ways. Illicit drugs are common in prisons, and syringes are difficult to come by so often they are shared, infecting many people. Unprotected sex is another risk factor in contracting AIDS—and according to the AIDS Foundation of Chicago, 65 percent of prisoners engage in sexual behaviors, and up to 28 percent are victims of sexual attacks. These figures might be higher, since not all prisoners report sexual abuse to officials.

Each year approximately 650,000 U.S. prisoners finish their sentences and return to society. Inmates with AIDS may return to risk-taking behaviors if they are not educated and do not have good support. This can be a hazard to society and to themselves, as they may decline in health or return to prison. When authorities deny prisoners their medications or cause them to miss treatments, serious consequences to the general population can occur. Cynthia Chandler, director of the Women's Positive Legal Action Network in Oakland, California, says, "It would not surprise me if we start finding large amounts of drug-resistant HIV as a result of people coming back into their communities after having been denied their medications while in prison."

THE "SILENT EPIDEMIC"

Hepatitis C (HCV) is now the most common blood-borne disease in the United States. Estimates are that four million U.S. citizens now have HCV, whereas less than one million have HIV infection. Prison populations in the United States have the highest concentration of HCV in the country, and 20 to 60 percent of inmates may be infected with the virus. Some researchers call HCV the silent epidemic, because often a person has no noticeable symptoms for up to twenty to thirty years after being infected; this means that most of those who have HCV do not know it.

The number of inmates with HCV surpasses HIV-infected inmates in Canadian prisons also. Studies done in the mid-1990s showed that between 28 and 40 percent of inmates were infected with HCV. In 2002, 3,173 inmates tested positive for HCV. In the prison population, 25.2 percent of male inmates and 33.7 percent of female inmates had the infection. Many prisoners come to prison already infected, but prison conditions make it easy to spread diseases further as HCV spreads more easily than HIV. HCV can lead to *cirrhosis*, liver disease, and liver cancer. There is no vaccine or proven cure.

Some state prisons in the United States avoid testing and treating HCV patients because costs to treat the illness are very high, sometimes as much as $25,000 a year. In 2000, the Texas Department of Corrections came up with a plan for testing, monitoring, and treating those with *chronic* infections, including HCV, and some other states say they give testing if requested. Jack Beck, a supervising attorney of the Prisoner's Rights Project of the Legal Aid Society in New York, says that if authorities release these prisoners without treatment, the end stages of this disease will be very expensive for public services to absorb.

GENERAL HEALTH CARE

In an article on the LifeExtension Web site, "Health of Our Prisons," Jon VanZile described his interviews with dozens of former prison inmates

PRISON CONDITIONS

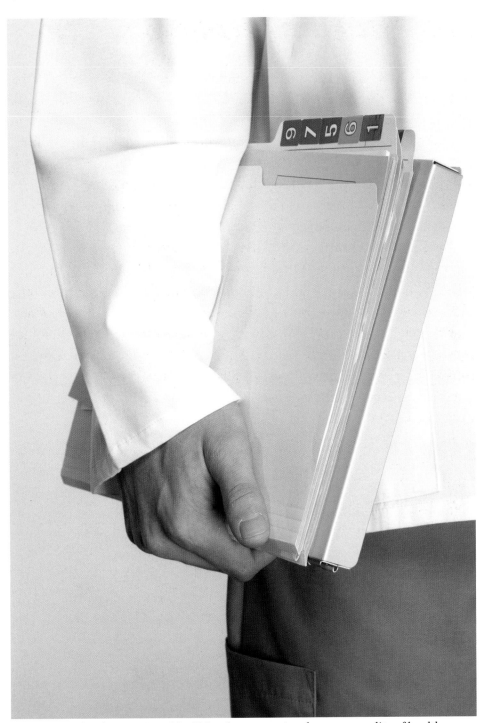

Inmates inside of correctional facilities do not receive the same quality of health care that they would on the outside.

Diabetic prisoners may not have access to adequate care for their condition.

concerning the quality of health care in U.S. prisons. Some rated the health-care services as very good, but unfortunately, this was not the typical response. Due to the closed nature of prisons, researchers have difficulty getting an accurate picture of what medical care is like. If any checks and balances exist, they usually come from the inside—and sometimes no one checks. Meanwhile, the inmate population suffers from higher levels of illness such as cancer, heart disease, and infectious diseases than those found in the general public. VanZile says that according to inmate accounts, they are regularly required to wait for medical care, and when they get it, it is "woefully inadequate."

In the United States, incarceration health care varies from state to state. In a recent report, California state prisons' medical departments have admitted to being in shambles. They have stated that in spite of spending two or three times as much as some other states on medical services, they have terrible medical facilities, and prisoners often die because of medical negligence and incompetent doctors. According to *San Francisco Chronicle* writer James Sterngold, some of the problems in the system include lack of nurses, doctors, and social workers to fill the job vacancies; prison salaries that are 30 to 40 percent lower than similar jobs in the public sector make these positions less attractive to employees. A report of San Quentin's facilities stated inmates had no privacy during medical examinations, the rooms were dirty, and the records were unorganized. California is planning on turning over its prison health care to an outside managed care provider sometime in the year 2006.

Marvin Johnson, whose story is told in the book *Prison Nation: The Warehousing of America's Poor*, was arrested on the morning of July 27, 1995, for driving an acquaintance's car without permission. When arrested, he told three nurses and six sheriff's deputies that he was an insulin-dependent diabetic and needed his medicine. His girlfriend called the main jail headquarters to inform officials of his diabetic needs. When she offered to bring his medications, the officials told her they would take good care of him. Later, the nurse in charge accused Johnson of "faking" his condition, and in the end, the jail staff never gave Johnson his necessary shots, saying that he was vague about his medical history and that they could not confirm his prescription.

Less than three days after his arrest, he fell into a coma and died. Correctional Medical Services (CMS) claims they did not get a report of Marvin's girlfriend calling the authorities. Annie Johnson, who helped to raise Johnson and his three siblings, sued the sheriff and CMS for medical malpractice, negligence, and wrongful death.

The company in charge of medical services at the jail where Marvin died was CMS—the largest health-care provider to jails and prisons in the United States. In June of 2000, CMS served more than 260,000 inmates in 315 prisons and jails in twenty-seven states. Unfortunately, CMS has many complaints against it for giving substandard medical care. It has a history of hiring doctors and other health-care workers with records of lawsuits filed against them for malpractice and sexual assaults. In many states, the practice of hiring doctors who have had their licenses revoked is common because such incompetent medical workers turn to prisons as their last resorts for employment. Many parties have filed

Justice should protect a prisoner's right to the same health care that the outside community receives.

lawsuits against CMS for wrongful deaths and lack of proper medical actions. In one rebuttal to a suit, a spokesperson stated that CMS was unfairly blamed for the problems of the jail. He claimed that inadequate funding for jail services, an old facility, and extreme overcrowding were to blame in the case.

Under the Eighth Amendment of the U.S. Constitution, prison authorities are required to give inmates adequate medical care known as the "community standard" of health care. In other words, prisons are required to give the same level of care the outside community gives itself. Federal, state, and local prison systems, however, have deteriorated because of the indifference of the general population, a huge prison population explosion, and budget cuts. Because of these issues, although many dedicated and sincere medical professionals work in prisons, many facilities lack adequate medical care.

Canada also recognizes the right of prisoners to the same health care as the outside community. In a report in April of 2004, Correctional Services Canada stated Canadian prisons must improve their medical care for incarcerated citizens. Prisons' health services are underdeveloped compared to the rest of the community, stated the report, and their inmates are a very "high-risk population" in regards to health. The report acknowledges the need for assistance from the outside community to help with prevention of illness and the overseeing and regulation of medical care in prisons.

North American prisons have complicated and interwoven problems. Just as overcrowding intensifies prisons' medical failures, overcrowding also contributes to another prison issue: violence.

CHAPTER 4

VIOLENCE

John King was a common burglar when he went to prison. While at a Texas state prison, however, he was forced to interact with the race-based prison gangs. He coped by joining one—a **white supremacist** group that taught him violence and racial hatred. On his release in 1998, he and two other men killed an African American man, James Byrd Jr., by dragging him behind a truck. His case illustrates an all-too common occurrence: prisoners incarcerated for nonviolent crimes often become violent people.

Prisoners generally have brief opportunities to exercise outside—but these intervals can also be occasions when violence takes place between prisoners.

A former inmate in Pennsylvania also learned violence while serving time in juvenile detention. Daily fights were normal, so he learned how to be aggressive, give orders, and fight his way to the top. When released, he used robbery to support himself, and he ended up shooting a man. He then served eighteen years for homicide.

Testimonies of violence in prisons are numerous in both the United States and Canada. Prisoners face *austere* and violent conditions. Guards must always be on the watch for their own safety. Male-on-male rape is common, and in the United States, racial gangs dominate inmate life. In U.S. prisons, inmate attacks on prison staff has risen 50 percent since the early 1990s.

The boredom of prison life can lead to violence.

In *The Oxford History of the Prison*, a prisoner writes of his daily routine: "A sense of impending danger is always with you; you must be careful to move around people rather than against them or through them, but with care and reasonable sense you can move safely enough." His life is not a constant experience of fights, threats, plots, and "shanks" (prison-made knives)—though he has to be constantly watching those around him. For this prisoner and many like him, the biggest problem is monotony and boredom. Every day is the same; the idleness and boredom of it all wears him down. In conditions like this, violence may provide prisoners with drama and even entertainment.

INMATE-ON-GUARD VIOLENCE

Sometimes in the course of guarding inmates, violence is inflicted on prison guards. While transporting ten high-risk prisoners back to admin-

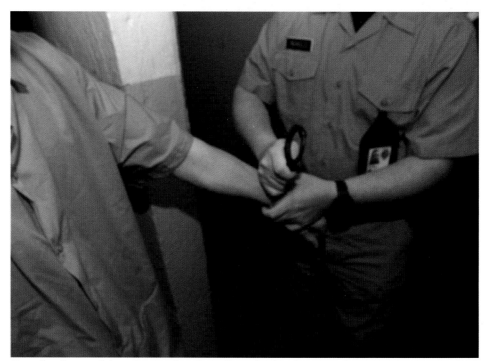
Guards who work in prisons often face the risk of violent attacks.

istrative segregation after working in a field at a Texas state jail, one of the prisoners stopped to converse with another employee about a disciplinary case. When the leading guard verbally admonished the prisoner to stay in line, the prisoner confronted the guard at the next round in the corridor. They were in an area with no video cameras, and the guard, feeling threatened, pushed the prisoner away. The other inmates began advancing toward the two, and the confronting prisoner hit the officer, causing his clipboard to open a long gash on his forehead. All the inmates then began chasing the guard, and he ran until he reached an area where other guards could see him and come to his aid.

Guards who have worked for many years in the system learn to "read" prisoners in order to avoid situations like this one. Prison staff usually know how to sense trouble before it happens and how to control cellblocks. Every day, guards hope to finish their shifts and go home without any problems.

INMATE-ON-INMATE VIOLENCE

In 1997, authorities arrested Aime Simard for three gang-related murders. Simard started serving his time in a British Columbia prison but then asked authorities to move him after he betrayed the Hell's Angels motorcycle gang, winning himself an early parole in spite of his serious crimes. According to CBC News, he feared for his life and thought that a prison in the province of Saskatchewan might be a safe place. Authorities moved him—but shortly after, on July 18, 2003, guards found him dead in his cell.

It is common for other inmates to kill an informant (a "snitch") in prison. Because of this, many violent incidents behind bars go unreported. Julian Sher, coauthor of a book on gangs, believes that authorities should have held Simard in protective custody, and an experienced corrections officer commented to CBC News that he was not surprised at the murder of Simard. The officer said that violence is on the rise in the

Maximum-security prisons are intended to curb gang activity.

Canadian prison system, and all penitentiaries are dangerous. Violence could break out at any time.

In the United States, many prisoners join a gang or a clique for protection. They must prove their eligibility first, but if they were in a gang on the outside or they are gang members from another prison, they are automatically eligible. Those who belong to gangs can be either a core member or an affiliate. Core members are the most active in gang activities; they rob other prisoners, control homosexual interactions, deal drugs, and fight with other gangs. The associates are not involved as closely with these activities, but they are ready if the gang needs a larger display of force, or to help in some operation such as smuggling drugs. Associates

Guards watch the prison yard for signs of violence.

have the protection of the gang and can walk more freely in prison public places.

Prison officials try to cut down on gang violence by determining which prisoners are gang leaders and core members, and putting them in maximum-security units. These prisoners may then stay there for many years. In Texas, for example, gang leaders stay in these "super-max" units until they have served their sentence. This practice has not totally stopped

A prison library; suspected gang members may not be allowed to use these facilities.

gang activity, however. Gang attacks and murders of other inmates and guards continue in the general prison population.

The majority of prisoners, especially those serving sentences for the first time, stay away from other prisoners and large gatherings of inmates. They stay with a few friends whom they may have met on their cellblocks, on the outside, in other prisons, or at their assigned prison work. Some choose to stay in their cells most of the time. Despite these practices, the number of gang members and associates rose in Saskatchewan, Canada, prisons during 1998–1999, according to an internal Saskatoon Correctional Centre report.

It's not easy to determine which violent incidents gangs caused. Each facility has a staff person designated to work with the area police and the Royal Mounted Canadian Police to identify and control gang members. According to a report by Inmate Services and Conditions of Custody, in Saskatchewan Correctional Centres, however, officials take several mea-

Sometimes prisoners must stay inside their cells if they want to avoid contact with gang members.

sures to cut down on possible gang violence. If an inmate is a known gang member, for example, he will not be able to get any work education training placement that may give status to gang membership. He cannot wear any gang-related items or keep property that endorses gang membership. Officials conduct frequent room and property checks to make sure inmates obtained their personal items through appropriate means, and officials also censor mail and telephone correspondence.

VIOLENCE

PRISON RAPE

Prison rape is an unpleasant subject that many in society choose to ignore. According to Lara Stemple, executive director of Stop Prison Rape (SPR), prison rape is an ***institutionalized atrocity*** that goes against a person's most basic human rights, causes the spread of disease, and creates a violent cycle both inside and outside prison walls.

A recent study done on four Midwestern state prisons reported that one in five male prisoners reported a forced or pressured sexual experience while in prison. According to a 2001 Human Rights Watch report, anywhere from 200,000 to 650,000 inmates (mostly males) are raped in the United States every year. Rates for female rape differ greatly between facilities, and the rapists are usually male staff workers. In one institution, 27 percent of the women reported a pressured or forced sexual incident. In another institution, no one reported any sexual misconduct, showing that prisons can prevent sexual harassment and rape.

Studies show that juveniles placed in adult prisons are five times more likely to be victims of sexual assault than youth in juvenile detentions. Many states are sentencing more and more youth offenders as adults, which results in growing amounts of abuse. According to SPR, the suicide rate is 7.7 times higher for young people in adult institutions than in youth detention centers.

Anyone can become a victim, but certain characteristics make some more vulnerable than others. Men incarcerated for the first time and nonviolent offenders are prime targets. Many of these have no gang affiliations to protect them and are not able to protect themselves. Prisoners often attack smaller, younger men who are somewhat feminine. Gay men are often targets. For women, specific characteristics do not play such a large part in deciding victims of abuse, but younger, first-time offenders and women who are mentally disabled are more likely targets.

Many times, male victims of rape become targets for more attacks. They accept sexual slavery to a powerful inmate in order to survive. Other prisoners treat them like property or force them into prostitution. For some, barbaric assaults by gangs or individuals have left them bleeding, beaten, and sometimes dead.

PRISON CONDITIONS

> *"The horrors experienced by many young inmates, particularly those who are convicted of nonviolent offenses, border on the unimaginable. Prison rape not only threatens the lives of those who fall prey to their aggressors, but it is potentially devastating to the human spirit. Shame, depression, and a shattering loss of self esteem accompany the perpetual terror the victim thereafter must endure."*
>
> —U.S. Supreme Court Justice Harry A. Blackmun, Farmer v. Brennan

Sexual assaults can be a death sentence to the victim if the rapist is infected with HIV or HCV. Women can end up pregnant and denied proper medical services. Some of the psychological effects are shock, insomnia, disbelief, anger, guilt, withdrawal, humiliation, and shame. Many prisoners go through long-term effects such as ongoing fear, flashbacks, substance abuse, ***posttraumatic stress disorder***, depression, anxiety, and suicide. Male survivors sometimes suppress their extreme anger over the incident until release from prison, when they become involved in antisocial and violent behavior in the community. Some become rapists themselves, trying to gain back a feeling of masculinity.

Prison rape is also very costly to the public. Expenses may involve lawsuits, reincarceration, ***recidivism***, and higher amounts of substance abuse, mental health services, and medical care for sexually transmitted diseases.

On September 4, 2003, President George W. Bush signed the Prison Rape Elimination Act. The law passed without opposition from the Senate or the Congress, and it created a nine-member National Prison Rape Reduction Commission to investigate and report on rape in U.S. prisons.

Women in prison are especially vulnerable to rape and sexual assault.

CBC News asked the question, "Do you think Canada's prisons are too soft?" Many wrote letters answering, yes. One young woman wrote the following:

> If you think that Canada's prisons are too soft . . . find a room that is about eight by six feet, move in your bed, some shelves, a small writing table, a TV, some books, a coffee maker, and with some luck, a chair. Put a toilet in the extra space left over, and hope that maybe you will have a window. Plan to stay there for at least two years. In most prisons, you get to come out of your room for meals and a half-hour each day for yard or library time.
>
> In the morning you get up to make sure someone did not rape you or stab you in your sleep. Someone opens your door for you—you can't just go and come as you please. As you are walking around, always be on your guard. Make sure to be careful whom you look at and how, it could get you killed. Don't express yourself too much and you might stay alive.

The act also gave funding to states to prevent prison rape and to prosecute accused prison rapists.

Prison overcrowding makes it difficult to provide simple rape prevention techniques such as grouping cellmates together according to risk. Rapes usually occur when no one is around to see or hear the event. Sometimes they happen at night in poorly lit places; inmates report that often their screams for help are unanswered. When prisoners report

The judicial system has not been particularly concerned about the issue of rape in prisons.

victimization by a rapist, the common procedure is to put the victim in administrative segregation, similar to solitary confinement. This is hard for most prisoners to endure, and this practice discourages them from reporting the crime.

The judicial system also appears to lack any concern about prison rape: many prosecutors are not interested in taking cases between inmates. They usually leave internal prison matters to prison authorities, who in turn do not often push for trials for inmate-on-inmate abuses. Authorities rarely punish rapists, whether they are prisoners or staff members. Some victims have reported that prison workers have retaliated

Rapes usually occur when there is no one around to see.

when the inmate filed a complaint against them. Prisons workers have used rape as a tool to punish some inmates, putting them in the same cell as known rapists and ignoring their pleas for help.

PRISON RIOTS

Prison riots usually happen in protest against prison conditions and when relations between inmates and prison officials break down. From 1971 to 1992, at least fourteen major prison riots took place in the United States. The two worst were at Attica, a New York State prison, in 1971, and at New Mexico State Penitentiary in 1980. In the Attica riot, state officers killed thirty-two unarmed prisoners and eleven prison employees. Four of the prison workers and all the inmates died of gunfire inflicted by police regaining control. Prison inmates killed thirty-three prisoners in the New Mexico riot. Many of the murdered prisoners had been in protective custody, and fellow prisoners thought they were informers.

Kingston Penitentiary in Canada was the site of one of Canada's largest riots. In 1971, inmates took over the facilities for four days, and rioters released 641 prisoners from their cellblocks. In the end, two inmates died, and the interior of the cellblock was destroyed. PrisonJustice.ca states that the riot was in reaction to the upcoming transfer of inmates and guards to Millhaven, the new, maximum-security prison. Rumors said this new facility had cells bugged so that guards could hear every word a prisoner said.

After the riot, Canadian officials established the Commission of Inquiry to start looking into the Kingston riot as well as several other disturbances at other penal institutions in the Canadian system. The commission found the need for a better way to address inmate complaints, and so the Office of the Correctional Investigator was formed to work on behalf of inmates.

Despite this step, inmates rioted at Kent Prison in British Columbia in 2003. The reason cited was the inmates' anger over recent changes at the institution: authorities had made new rules banning group meetings

PRISON CONDITIONS

of prisoners, enforcing the wearing of prison uniforms, and making all inmates eat inside their cells. One prisoner died in the struggle.

In Manitoba, Canada, the correction facilities use a system that attempts to measure the *volatility* of the environment. Staff members fill out a checklist reporting any increases in telephone calls, hand signals, canteen purchases, requests for protection, and visitor cancellations, along with any decreases in communications, eye contact, and prisoner participation in programs. Changes in these activities may indicate a violent event is brewing.

Riots seem to happen more often in the larger, overcrowded prisons where there is idleness and racial tension. Gangs are often the cause of riots. Sometimes a harsh environment makes the prison like a bomb "waiting to explode." All too often, abuse plays a major role in the explosion.

VIOLENCE

CHAPTER 5

ABUSE

In Texas, a thirty-one-year-old man diagnosed with schizo-phrenia had a psychotic episode on the night of July 6, 1999. Delusional and believing that a relative was chasing and trying to murder him, he ran to the police for safety. Unfortunately, this was not his safest option, and by the end of the night, he was dead.

Guard brutality is a fact of life in many prisons.

According to *Prison Nation: The Warehousing of America's Poor*, the police sprayed the delusional man with pepper spray and then put him in a restraining chair. Police did not allow him to wash the spray out of his eyes or face, which is a violation of department procedures. His mother's lawyer stated, "He was not decontaminated, and he was left alone in a room. Within twenty minutes he was dead."

Although many detention officers, police, and prison staff may be dedicated to the welfare of inmates, some are all too prone to abusive

Pepper spray is often misused by prison guards.

behavior. Amnesty International has been telling the U.S. Congress for many years that cruelty does not just happen in other countries; it is happening in U.S. prisons today. National awareness is growing as stories of prison brutality eventually make their way to public knowledge.

FURNITURE MISUSE

The electric chair is not the only dreaded chair in penitentiaries and jails. Some prison employees have called the other chair the "we care chair," the "be sweet chair," the "strap-o-lounger," and the "barca-lounger." Some inmates and their lawyers call it "slave chair," "torture chair," and "devil's chair." It is a restraining chair intended for the most violent prisoners. Testimonies of prisoners and lawyers, as well as reviews of jail videotapes, court cases, and scattered news stories, report that the restraint chair is being used improperly and sometimes in a **sadistic** manner.

In the 1999 Texas case, the manufacturers of the police department's chair, KLK, Inc., of Phoenix, called their product a "Violent Person Restraint Chair." They are proud to say that it had been used by a very large jail system for four years, with a 90 percent reduction of injuries

compared to the previous four years. KLK sells these chairs mainly to prisons and hospitals, and it insists that the chair is not responsible for anyone's death: the issue is how the chair is used. Meanwhile, however, an attorney in Atlanta claims that the mere presence of any restraint chair is asking for abuse.

Prison Nation says authorities have used restraint chairs for children who were demonstrating nonviolent but annoying behavior. Officials have also used these chairs on adult detainees and inmates for up to eight days at a time. Inmates have been tortured while pepper sprayed and hooded, forced to testify, interrogated, threatened, or beaten. Some prisoners have been strapped in a restraint chair in the nude. In the United States, at least eleven people have died after being strapped into these chairs—and yet the chair has become popular in U.S. jails, federal and state prisons, juvenile detention centers, the U.S. Citizenship and Immigration Services, state mental hospitals, and the U.S. Marshals Service.

In late 1996, a former journalist died at the Connecticut Valley Hospital after authorities held her for thirty-three hours in a restraint chair in a local jail. When they released her, blood clots that had formed in her legs traveled to her lungs, killing her.

A Maricopa County, Arizona, man died in June of 1996 after prison guards gagged him, pushed him into a restraint chair, forced his head to his chest, and shocked him with a stun gun. The county coroner said his death was an accident, but the courts later ruled that the man's death was a direct result of his time spent in the restraint chair.

The Sacramento, California, sheriff's department settled a lawsuit claiming that deputies were torturing people with a restraint chair. According to former inmates, the guards strapped prisoners in the chair and told them they would electrocute them. A 106-pound woman claimed to have been strapped in the chair for eight and a half hours with the restraining straps so tight they cut off circulation in her legs and arms, and sliced the skin from her back and shoulders. She alleges that prison workers mocked and taunted her while they denied her water or use of the bathroom.

Canada, meanwhile, has only six restraint chairs as of 2003. Officials use the chair at times for suicidal inmates or those high on drugs. John

PRISON CONDITIONS

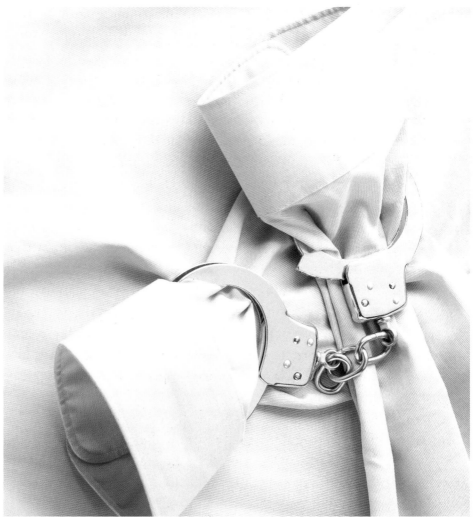

Using a strait jacket is another form of prison restraint.

Schofield, Newfoundland's superintendent of prisons, says prison workers use the chairs solely for the protection of the prisoner or the other prisoners—but according to a prisoner rights advocate with the John Howard Society, former inmates say differently. They say guards use it as a form of punishment.

In the United States, there are efforts to ban or restrict the use of the restraint chair. In 1999, a Knox County, Tennessee, judge ruled the confession of a robbery suspect was involuntary and illegal because

ABUSE

A restraint chair

authorities had held him for five hours in a restraint chair. Amnesty International has called for a review of the use of restraint chairs in jails and prisons based on evidence of its misuse. A criminal court judge stated that while the restraint chair might be useful, it could easily cross the line into being a coercive force.

CHEMICAL SPRAYS AND ELECTRIC SHOCKS

Pictures of torture at Abu Ghraib, a prison in Baghdad, Iraq, shocked the world in 2004. Deborah Davies, a British reporter for the BBC, channel 4, conducted a four-month investigation on prisons in the United States to see if there was an explanation for American's actions in Iraq. She obtained videos of prisoners experiencing what she calls "wholesale torture" inside U.S. prisons. She did not base her findings on rumors or hearsay but on solid evidence from videos from all across the United States. In many states, when guards need to exert force, they are required to videotape the event to prove they did not use excessive force—but many tapes prove the opposite.

Multiple lawyers who spoke to Deborah Davies agreed that abuse in U.S. prisons happens all the time. One lawyer pointed as proof to mountains of files stacked on his desk and floor, files filled with stories of alarming treatment inside U.S. prisons. Davies got her videotapes from lawyers who got them from reluctant state prisons for use during drawn-out lawsuits.

Pepper spray and electric taser guns are two methods of "controlling" prisoners. An Amnesty International 1998 report details the *caustic* effects of pepper spray: The mucous membranes of the eyes, nose, and mouth become inflamed, causing the eyes to close. The victim experiences shortness of breath, gagging, coughing, and a terrible burning sensation on the skin and inside the mouth and nose. The effects are extremely unpleasant.

Many times guards use pepper spray for trivial reasons. Deborah Davies found that some of the reasons for spraying inmates include banging on their doors and refusing medications. Prisoners report telltale signs that guards are about to spray them: prison workers place cardboard under their door to make sure the room is airtight, while they cut off ventilation fans. One lawyer explained that guards usually use fire-extinguisher–size canisters full of pepper spray. He has seen prisoners with

Pepper spray is literally made from hot peppers. Imagine what it would feel like to have the juice from these peppers sprayed in your eyes!

second-degree burns from the pepper spray all over their bodies. Some have been sprayed and "left to cook in the burning fog of chemicals." One lawyer showed Davies pictures of his client with a large burned patch on his hip. Another photo showed an inmate with a terrible rash across his neck, back, and arms.

The pepper spray used by prison guards often comes in canisters the size of fire extinguishers—which means that dangerous amounts can be sprayed on inmates.

In January of 2005, two prisoners died in Alabama. One was pepper sprayed and one was tasered. A tape from Florida also shows a prisoner tasered for refusing orders. As he lies on an examining table, the guards instruct him to climb down into a wheelchair. He yells, "I can't, I can't!" and, "It hurts!" A guard then jabs him on both hips with a taser. As the electricity hits him, the man jerks and screams but he still will not get into the chair. The guards grab him and force him into the chair. When they try to bend his legs to fit the footrest, he shrieks in pain. The video ends showing the guards trying to make the prisoner walk with a walker. He falls on the floor crying in pain, and they taser him again. He finally lays there moaning because he has run out of energy and breath to cry. The man's lawyer told Davies that his client had a very limited mental capacity, plus he had a back problem that caused him to have terrible pain when he walked or bent his legs.

A German concentration camp, where the bodies of tortured and murdered inmates were burned; the camp guards may have learned cruelty and violence from their environment.

GUARD ABUSE OF INMATES

Officials regarded it as one of the foremost high-tech prisons in the United States when it was first built in 1993. The Federal Correctional Complex in Florence, Colorado, had lower security facilities, a maximum-security unit, and an administrative maximum-security facility. It also had brutal guards who called themselves the Cowboys. Due to media exposure, complaints from other prison staff, and many lawsuits filed by inmates, in 1999, the public got a view of how the guards at Florence abused prisoners.

EXCESSIVE FORCE

Scholars argue whether corruption and cruelty among guards is due to the conditions they see every day in their workplace or is something that springs from their own personalities. Victor Hassine, author of Life Without Parole, has seen firsthand that personalities change in prison. He believes that "even the gentlest person in the world will become violent after spending five years in a prison like Graterford. . . . What goes for prisoners also goes for prison staff." Hassine thinks it is logical that if understaffed and overcrowded prisons teach criminality, rage, and violence to inmates, they will also affect the staff that spends much of their waking hours in the same environment.

Prison Nation tells how guards at Florence bashed the heads of inmates into walls, kicked them, and mixed feces and urine into their food. Once, two guards threw a burning piece of paper into a cell to justify spraying the men inside with a fire extinguisher. Many prisoners suffered at the hands of these men.

The Cowboys formed in 1995 as a secret gang of disgruntled guards. They believed that prisoners assigned to the Special Housing Unit (SHU) for attacking staff were punished too lightly—so they decided to kick, hit, and torture cuffed and chained prisoners, and then falsely document that the prisoners provoked the violence. The Cowboys threatened physical harm to officers who stood up to them in defense of inmates. A former Florence guard said he and others told management about the abuse many times, but management did nothing to stop it.

A court indicted seven members of the Cowboys, charging them with fifty-two acts of misconduct.

On November 2, 2000, a court *indicted* seven members of the Cowboys, charging them with fifty-two acts of misconduct against twenty specific prisoners from 1995 to 1997. The attorney representing the guards claimed that the prisoners trumped up false charges. The president of the local union stood up for the accused guards, saying they had been good guards. The former union leaders who blew the whistle on the Cowboys to the Bureau of Prisons were not elected the following term. The candidate who won denied that anything wrong happened. He had the union set up a fund for the families of accused guards while the case was pending. If not for the undaunted reports of a local writer and the guards who

Guard union leaders created a fund to help pay for the defense of the accused guards.

The relationship between guard and prisoner is not always abusive.

A good relationship between prison staff and inmates results in better conditions for both sides of the equation.

testified against their cohorts, the abuse at Florence might have continued.

Of course not all prison guards are abusive. A great many prison workers fulfill the duties of their difficult work with professionalism, and some go beyond that, showing genuine care for inmates. Author Victor Hassine was surprised at how well guards and inmates generally got along at his Pennsylvania prison. He found no open hostility between the two groups; instead, many officials and prisoners went out of their way to make good relationships. If good relationships were established, both inmates and guards knew they would benefit. Inmates hoped for special benefits such as increased shower time or an extra phone call, and guards hoped for easy-to-handle prisoners and their personal safety.

Women inmates often face discrimination.

NATIVE POPULATIONS IN PRISON

"Aboriginal people [North American Indians] are over-represented in Canadian prison facilities," says PrisonJustice.ca. In 1999, Canada incarcerated 735 per 100,000 Aboriginal people, whereas the national average was 151 per 100,000 people. Aboriginal women make up 27 percent of women serving time in federal prisons, while they make up less than 2 percent of the Canadian population.

FEMALE INMATES

Some Canadians feel that prison facilities discriminate against women. Women are a small group of prisoners who do not usually need maximum-security facilities, yet officials place most of them in high-security facilities anyway. Women do not have the same accessibility to programs, **halfway houses**, family contact, or education. They need specialized medical care such as gynecological, prenatal, and postnatal care. Women also need their own services for overcoming drug and alcohol abuse, and they need counseling provided by women to help with abuse issues. Because women are more often responsible for the care of both parents in their elderly years and young children, incarcerated women need parenting services.

In 2000, the Prison for Women closed in Kingston, Ontario, and the government shipped women to isolated areas of men's prisons. Since

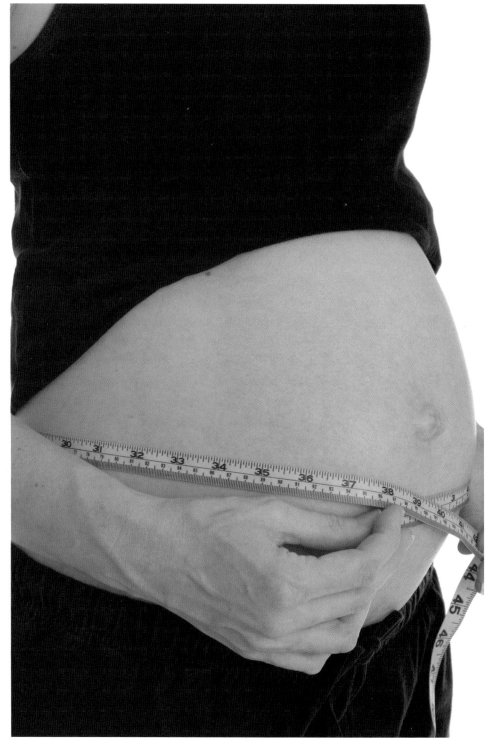

Pregnancy puts a woman prisoner at increased risk.

then, the rates of women prisoners' suicide attempts and self-destruction has gone up. "Women try to find a way out of these inhumane conditions, even through death," one female prisoner shared on PrisonJustice.ca.

In Canada, according to some concerned citizens, certain women are especially at risk in prisons. Kim Pate, the executive director of the Canadian Association of Elizabeth Fry Societies, believes that prisons especially discriminate against Aboriginal women and women with disabilities. The Disabled Women's Network Canada believes that authorities are discriminating against federally sentenced females with mental and developmental disabilities. Officials see mental disability as a danger. If a woman is suicidal or has cognitive or mental disabilities, authorities might put her in isolation, without clothes, in a barren cell. The prison has become a substitute for community-based mental health services. In 2003, the Prisoner's Justice Day Committee, along with women's groups and prisoner's rights groups across Canada, asked the Correctional Service of Canada as well as the government of Canada to end the discriminating treatment of women in prison and to close the new maximum-security prisons for women.

Female inmates in the United States sometimes go through the appalling experience of being pregnant while in prison. Two women in a Michigan facility told Amnesty International that officials took them to the hospital in a belly chain and handcuffs. One of the women had her legs shackled together. Officials removed her restraints just before the birth of her child only at the insistence of the doctor, but the guard had to get permission from the prison first. Guards handcuffed the other woman to the bed until the baby was just about to be born and again handcuffed both women to their beds immediately after they gave birth.

The female inmates confided in Amnesty International that in spite of an investigation by the U.S. Justice Department into sexual abuse of female inmates in Michigan and the consequent legal action that took place, guards were still sexually abusing female inmates. The inmates said that guards watched women in the showers or when dressing, sexually assaulted them, and touched them inappropriately during pat searches. They also told of inadequate medical attention. Amnesty International spoke with two female guards who confirmed the stories that sexual

Inside prison fences, a multitude of problems wait to be handled.

abuse is a pattern in female incarceration units. If the female inmates complained, they were threatened or punished. One guard reported that she was harassed after she complained about the sexual behavior of the guards, and eventually, she was beaten and slashed. Amnesty International has heard the same sort of reports from inmates in some other states as well.

CONCLUSION

The conditions inside of some Canadian and U.S. prisons and jails are not a pretty picture. Overcrowding, violence, abuse, and disease are all too common. As thousands of inmates rejoin the free world every day, are they coming back to us more broken than when they went to prison? Have prison conditions left them scarred and useless to society? Some victims feel that punishment is all prisoners deserve: shouldn't they feel as much pain as those whose lives they have damaged? Prison guards struggle to keep a sense of compassion in an environment where prisoners lie to them and challenge them constantly. Yet some social experts point out that the majority of convicts were sentenced to jail for nonviolent crimes, and they urge emphasis on rehabilitation rather than mere punishment.

What is best for prisoners? For victims? For society? These are important decisions that you and other citizens must make in the years ahead.

GLOSSARY

atrocity: Something that is evil or extremely cruel.

austere: Severely plain and simple.

authoritarian: Having to do with a system of strict rules in which obedience to a ruling person or group is strictly enforced.

berated: Scolded someone vigorously and lengthily.

bipolar disorder: A psychological disorder characterized by periods of extreme happiness alternating with extreme depression.

blatant: So obvious that it is impossible to hide.

boot camp: A disciplinary facility in which youthful offenders are forced to participate in a rigidly enforced routine.

caustic: Corrosive.

chronic: Something that is long term or recurs frequently.

cirrhosis: A chronic, progressive disease of the liver.

coerce: To force someone to do something he or she does not want to do.

complacent: Self-satisfied without being aware of possible dangers.

degradation: Great humiliation.

disposition: Settlement of a legal matter.

electronic monitoring: An incarceration alternative in which an electric positioning monitoring device is placed on the offender, telling authorities where he or she is at all times.

enigma: Someone or something that is not easily understood or explained.

extortion: The crime of obtaining something from someone using illegal methods of persuasion.

geriatric: Concerned with senior citizens.

halfway houses: Residences designed to ease people back into society after their release from an institution.

house arrest: The sentencing of an offender to remain in his or her home, or within a specified area, except for work or approved appointments.

PRISON CONDITIONS

indicted: Formally charged someone with a crime.

institutionalized atrocity: Became established as custom or an accepted part of the larger structure.

jail diversion programs: Programs for people with mental illness or co-occurring disorders who have been arrested for minor violations.

lynch mob: A group of people who capture and hang someone without legal arrest and trial.

paranoids: People who are obsessively suspicious of others.

posttraumatic stress disorder: A psychological condition that may affect people who have suffered severe emotional trauma.

probation: The supervision of the behavior of a young or first-time criminal by an officer of the court.

rail: To denounce, protest against, or attack someone or something in bitter or harsh language.

recidivism: To commit a crime again after release from prison.

rehabilitate: To help someone return to good standing in the community.

restitution: Compensation for a loss.

sadistic: Finding pleasure in inflicting physical or emotional pain on others.

schizophrenia: A psychological disorder characterized with a loss of contact with reality.

sociopaths: People whose behavior is antisocial and who lack a conscience.

stigmatized: Characterized by shame.

twelve-step groups: Programs for addiction recovery based on the methods of Alcoholics Anonymous and self-improvement techniques.

volatility: The ability to change suddenly.

weekend sentencing: Offenders are incarcerated only on weekends.

white supremacist: Someone who believes that whites are innately superior to others and, therefore, entitled to dominate the lesser groups.

FURTHER READING

Bartollas, Clemens, and Katherine Stuart van Wormer. *Women and the Criminal Justice System*. Needham Heights, Mass.: Allyn & Bacon, 2000.

Edgar, Kathleen. *Youth Violence, Crime, and Gangs: Children at Risk.* Farmington Hills, Mich.: Gale, 2004.

Espejo, Roman, editor. *America's Prisons: Opposing Viewpoints*. San Diego, Calif.: Greenhaven Press, 2002.

Ferro, Jeffrey. *Crime: A Serious American Problem*. Farmington Hills, Mich.: Gale, 2003.

Hassine, Victor. *Life Without Parole: Living in Prison Today*. Los Angeles, Calif.: Roxbury Publishing Company, 2000.

Herivel, Tara, and Paul Wright, editors. *Prison Nation: The Warehousing of America's Poor*. New York: Routledge, 2003.

Laci, Miklos. *Prisons and Jails: A Deterrent to Crime?* Farmington Hills, Mich.: Gale, 2004.

Lerner, Jimmy. *You Got Nothing Coming: Notes from a Prison Fish*. New York: Broadway Books, 2002.

Rabiger, Joanna. *Daily Prison Life*. Broomall, Pa.: Mason Crest Publishers, 2003.

Richards, Stephen C., and Jeffrey Ian Ross. *Behind Bars: Surviving Prison*. Indianapolis, Ind.: Alpha Books, 2002.

Rolef, Tamara L., editor. *Criminal Justice: Opposing Viewpoints*. Farmington Hills, Mich.: Greenhaven Press, 2003.

PRISON CONDITIONS

FOR MORE INFORMATION

AIDS Foundation of Chicago: addressing the intersection of HIV/AIDS and Prison-HIV statistics
www.aidschicago.org/advocacy/2005_priorities_prisons.php

Canada—History of Prison Justice Day
www.prisonjustice.ca/prisonjustice/politics/1014_history.html

Encyclopedia of Criminology in Canada
www.routledge-ny.com/ref/criminology/canada.html

Human Rights Watch
hrw.org/english/docs/2004/10/22/usdom9558.htm

Inmate Services and Conditions of Custody—Saskatchewan
www.legassembly.sk.ca/officers/omb/Locked_Out/
02%20Living%20Cond.pdf

Origins of Prisons as Agencies of Punishment
www.notfrisco.com/prisonhistory/origins/index.html

PBS, Prisons in America—Bill Moyer
www.pbs.org/now/society/prisons3.html

Prison Justice.caDiscrimination against women in prison
www.prisonjustice.ca/politics/1012_failedexp.html

Statistics, Bureau of Justice
www.ojp.usdoj.gov/bjs/prisons.htm

Publisher's note:
The Web sites listed on this page were active at the time of publication. The publisher is not responsible for Web sites that have changed their addresses or discontinued operation since the date of publication. The publisher will review and update the Web-site list upon each reprint.

BIBLIOGRAPHY

Aids Foundation of Chicago.
    http://www.aidschicago.org/advocacy/2005_priorities_prisons.php.

Bureau of Justice, http://www.ojp.usdoj.gov/bjs/prisons.htm.

Canadian Church Council on Justice and Corrections. http://www.ccjc.ca.

Canadian Criminal Justice Association.
    http://www.ccja-acjp.ca/en/overc2.html.

CBC. "Are Canadian Prisons Too Soft?"
    http://www.cbc.ca/prison/letters2.html.

Correctional Service Canada. http://www.csc-scc.gc.ca.

Encyclopedia of Criminology in Canada.
    http://www.routledge-ny.com/ref/criminology/canada.html.

HIV treatment conditions in Canada.
    http://www.aidslaw.ca/Maincontent/issues/prisons/e-info-pa8.htm.

Human Rights Watch.
    http://hrw.org/english/docs/2004/10/22/usdom9558.htm.

Inmate Services and Conditions of Custody. http://www.legassembly.sk.ca/officers/
    omb/Locked_Out/11%20Aboriginal.pdf

LexisNexis U.S. Politics and World News.
    http://www6.lexisnexis.com/publisher/EndUser?Action=UserDisplayFullDocument
    &orgId=574&topicId=27010&docId=l:272769922&start=1.

Prison justice in Canada. http://www.prisonjustice.ca/prisonjustice/politics/1014_
    history.html.

PsychLinks Online. http://www.psychlinks.ca/phpbb/viewtopic.php?p=7612&.

Stop Prison Rape. http://www.spr.org/en/reductionactstatement.html.

Stories of rape in prison, http://www.spr.org.

Ted Conover, http://www.tedconover.com/jailer.html#top.

PRISON CONDITIONS

INDEX

PICTURE CREDITS

PRISON CONDITIONS

Chapter opening art was taken from a painting titled *HCV in Prison Bird Cage* by Raymond Gray.

Raymond Gray has been incarcerated since 1973. Mr. Gray has learned from life, and hard times, and even from love. His artwork reflects all of these.

BIOGRAPHIES

AUTHOR

Roger Smith holds a degree in English education and formerly taught in the Los Angeles public schools. Smith did volunteer work with youthful inmates at a juvenile detention facility in Los Angeles. He currently lives in Arizona.

SERIES CONSULTANT

Dr. Larry E. Sullivan is Associate Dean and Chief Librarian at the John Jay College of Criminal Justice and Professor of Criminal Justice in the doctoral program at the Graduate School and University Center of the City University of New York. He first became involved in the criminal justice system when he worked at the Maryland Penitentiary in Baltimore in the late 1970s. That experience prompted him to write the book *The Prison Reform Movement: Forlorn Hope* (1990; revised edition 2002). His most recent publication is the three-volume *Encyclopedia of Law Enforcement* (2005). He has served on a number of editorial boards, including the *Encyclopedia of Crime and Punishment,* and *Handbook of Transnational Crime and Justice.* At John Jay College, in addition to directing the largest and best criminal justice library in the world, he teaches graduate and doctoral level courses in criminology and corrections. John Jay is the only liberal arts college with a criminal justice focus in the United States. Internationally recognized as a leader in criminal justice education and research, John Jay is also a major training facility for local, state, and federal law enforcement personnel.